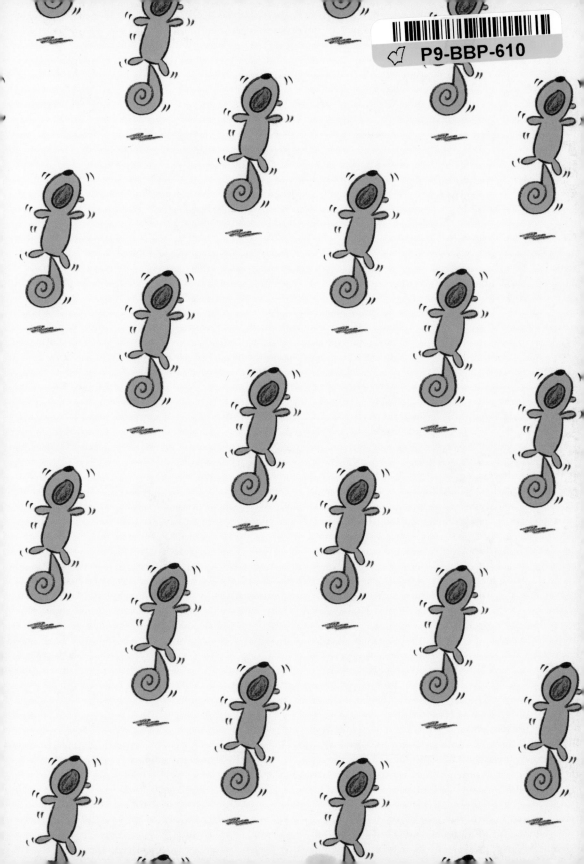

For Oom Robbie

First Edition, June 2008
15 14 13 12 11 10
FAC-029191-16032

Library of Congress Cataloging-in-Publication Data on file.
ISBN: 978-1-4231-0962-4

Visit www.hyperionbooksforchildren.com and www.pigeonpresents.com

I Will Surprise My Friend!

An **ELEPHANT & PIGGIE** Book

By **Mo Willems**

Hyperion Books for Children/New York

AN IMPRINT OF DISNEY BOOK GROUP

Hee hee hee!

4

Shhh . . .
Here she
comes!

5

6

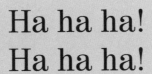

8

We could surprise each other!

We could surprise each other by the big rock!

27

Where can my friend be?

31

33

. . . a giant bird grabbed
Piggie and flew off
with her!

... a scary, scary
monster is trying
to eat her right now!

44

46

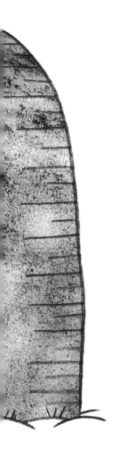

That was a surprise.

A big surprise.

PLONK!

55

Deal.

Elephant and Piggie have more funny adventures in: